Sheryl Griffin

By Dandi Daley Mackall

Illustrated by Glin Dibley

Zonderkidz

To my husband, Joe, and to Jen, Katy, and Dan—my family. I love you guys.
—DDM

Being surrounded by girls is not so bad. . .
I dedicate this to my four girls, Liane, Kendra, Sawyer (and Duchess too),
whom I deeply love and adore.
—GD

Zonderkidz®
The children's group of Zondervan

www.zonderkidz.com

Made for a Purpose

Requests for information should be addressed to:
Zonderkidz, Grand Rapids, Michigan 49530

Library of Congress Cataloging-in-Publication Data

Mackall, Dandi Daley.
Made for a purpose / by Dandi Daley Mackall ; illustrated by Glin Dibley
p. cm.
Summary: Since her mother left, C.J. Jones does not do friends and does not smile, but as she builds sandcastles and dreams of becoming an architect, she notices a group of neighborhood children who invite her to play with them and tell her about God.
ISBN 0-310-70953-9 (hardcover)
[1. Friendship--Fiction. 2. Sandcastles--Fiction. 3. Architecture--Fiction. 4. Christian life--Fiction. 5. Beaches--Fiction.]
I. Dibley, Glin, ill. II. Title.
PZ7.M1905Mad 2004
[Fic]--dc22 2004008750

Editor: Amy DeVries
Art Direction and Design: Laura M. Maitner

Printed in Mexico
04 05 06 07/DR/4 3 2 1

Foreword

C.J. might be like some of your friends or even a little like you. She has a BIG hurt in her life that makes it hard for her to trust people. She doesn't know God created her to love her and shaped her with a specific purpose in mind. He gave her the eyes, nose, hair, brain, and personality he wanted her to have in order to fulfill her purpose in life.

You were created for a purpose too, and I pray this book will help you understand just how unique and specially designed you are: nothing about you is an accident! God gave you the parents he wanted you to have, made you look the way he wanted you to look, and gave you the interests you have so that you can do what he created you to do!

After you read this book, I hope you'll be glad God made you for a purpose. Then you'll be ready to begin a lifetime of discovering God's purpose for your life. It's the most exciting and adventurous journey – becoming what God made you to be!

Rick Warren
author of *The Purpose-Driven® Life*

C.J. hurried past the clubhouse where neighborhood kids met for some kind of Bible club.

Well, *she* had something a lot better than *their* stupid club. C.J. Jones was president and only member of the C.J. Jones Club, and she planned to keep it that way. She'd learned one thing when her mother walked out on Dad and her—trust yourself and nobody else.

As soon as she smelled salt air, C.J. raced the rest of the way to the beach. She couldn't wait to build beautiful sand castles. One day, she would be a famous architect, a person who drew pictures of buildings, then made the buildings. Her mother had taught her the word, *architect*. C.J. could still remember her mom talking about skyscrapers in New York, where Mom lived now.

C.J. arrived at her secret hideout on the deserted end of the beach. The old lifeguard stand rose like a skyscraper through the uneven sand. Checking to make sure nobody was watching, she slid a loose board to the side, then ducked in. On the sandy floor, she finished drawing the design of her castle.

Then C.J. hauled water from the ocean for her sand masterpiece. She imagined being watched by a famous architect, who would admire her castle and hire her on the spot.

When C.J. was back in her hideout, *she* heard voices coming from *her* end of the beach.

"Here's a good spot. Ace! Yushi!"

C.J. peeked out and saw Nick Rodriguez, one of those Bible kids.

She held her breath and stayed silent as sand.

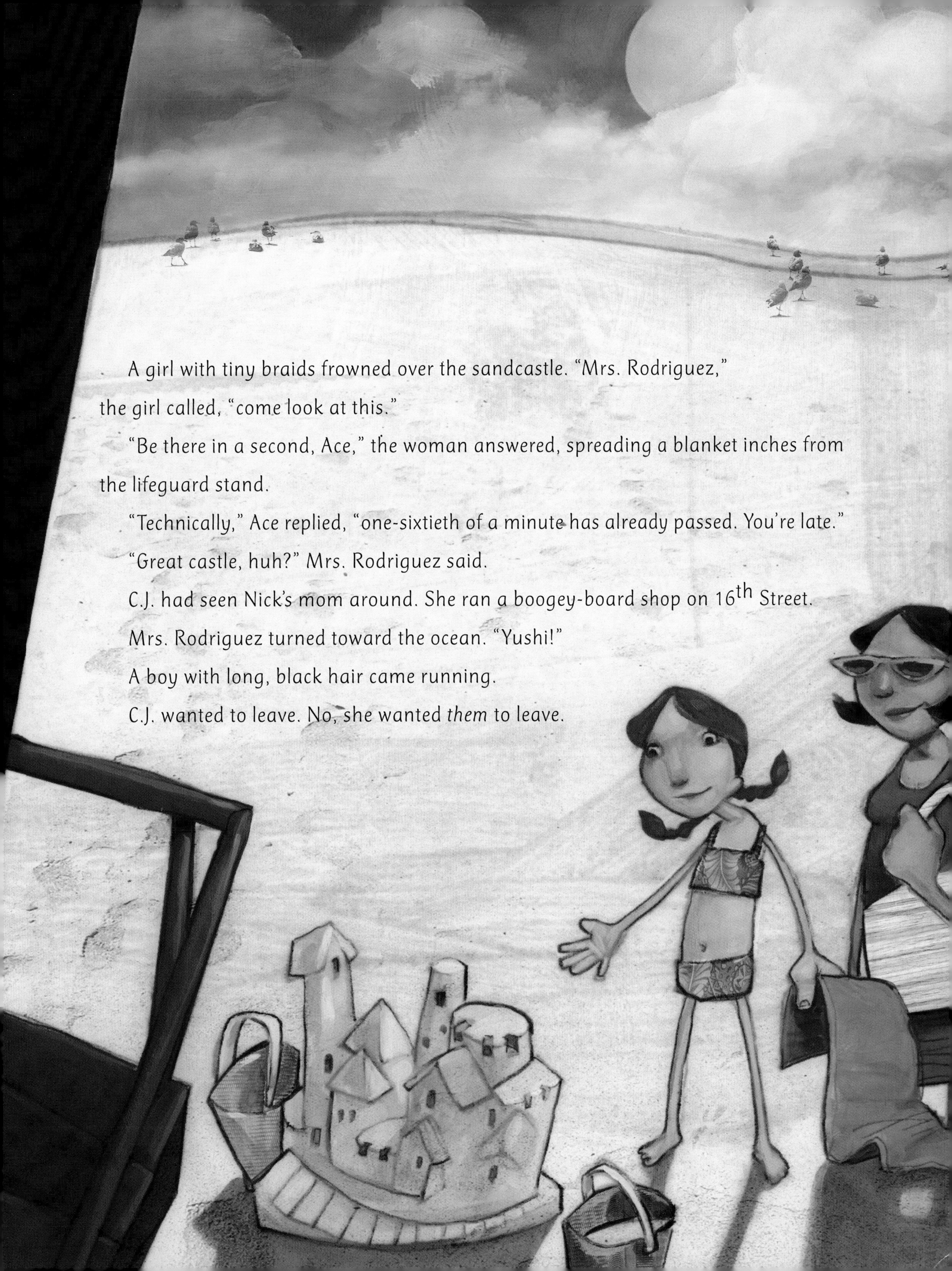

A girl with tiny braids frowned over the sandcastle. "Mrs. Rodriguez," the girl called, "come look at this."

"Be there in a second, Ace," the woman answered, spreading a blanket inches from the lifeguard stand.

"Technically," Ace replied, "one-sixtieth of a minute has already passed. You're late."

"Great castle, huh?" Mrs. Rodriguez said.

C.J. had seen Nick's mom around. She ran a boogey-board shop on 16th Street.

Mrs. Rodriguez turned toward the ocean. "Yushi!"

A boy with long, black hair came running.

C.J. wanted to leave. No, she wanted *them* to leave.

But they settled onto the blanket, and Mrs. Rodriguez read to them. It reminded C.J. of a long time ago, when her mom used to read fairytales to her. Only *this* book was about God.

C.J. wanted to sneak out, but she was trapped.

She tried not to listen. But they were so close.

"Does anyone know what God wants you to do with your life?" Mrs. Rodriguez asked.

C.J. waited for Nick's mom to come down on him.

But Mrs. Rodriguez laughed. "Could be."

"Okay," Nick said. "How about a lifeguard who loves God and wants to be his friend?"

Nick's mom smiled at his answer. She made it sound like all God wanted was to love you. C.J. wondered when they'd get to the part about not ticking God off. She was pretty sure there was more to this God story than love.

As she listened, C.J. doodled in the sand.

"Mrs. Rodriguez!" Ace shouted. "God also wants us to be part of his forever family."

Family? C.J. thought. *What's so forever about family?*

"Yushi, anything else?" Mrs. Rodriguez asked.

Yushi sat up. "I helped Mrs. Jackson, next door, carry in her groceries."

"Great!" Mrs. Rodriguez said. "Definitely something God wants us to do."

C.J. knew exactly what *she* wanted to do with her life.

"We don't want to forget that everybody needs Jesus, right?" Mrs. Rodriguez said. "Why don't we start praying for the whole world?"

Great, C.J. thought. *That's all I need. Now I'll never get out of here.*

Suddenly, Yushi jumped to his feet. "Come back here, you crazy seagull!"

"Guess we're done," Mrs. Rodriguez said. But she didn't sound mad, not like C.J.'s dad would've been.

"Look! I'm a lifeguard!" Nick shouted.

Sand filtered through the ceiling, and C.J. heard Nick thump around on *her* lifeguard stand. She wanted to climb up and throw him down.

Behind her, the secret board moved to the side. Then before C.J. realized what was happening, in came Yushi.

“Got you!” Yushi cried, as the gull scurried past him, just out of reach. Empty-handed, Yushi stood up. “Ahh!” he screamed when he saw C.J.

Then into the secret hideout came Ace and Mrs. Rodriguez, followed by Nick.

C.J. thought about making a run for it, but Nick was blocking the only exit.

Ace stepped forward. “Don’t mind Yushi. He’s scared of his own shadow.”

“Am not!” Yushi snapped.

“Nothing to be ashamed of, Yushi,” Ace said. “Even Edison was afraid of the dark—which explains why he invented the light bulb!”

Mrs. Rodriguez turned to C.J. and smiled. “We didn’t mean to disturb you… Cynthia, isn’t it?”

“C.J.,” she muttered. Nobody but her mother called her “Cynthia.”

“Want to join us, C.J.?” Mrs. Rodriguez asked, moving toward the exit.

“No thanks.” C.J. couldn’t believe these people expected her to join their Bible study, just like that. “I don’t do groups, and I don’t do friends.”

Nick laughed. “And you don’t smile, right?”

C.J. frowned. “Right.”

“Mom just asked if you wanted to walk home with us,” Nick explained.

C.J. felt the blood rush to her cheeks.

"Humans are the only creatures who blush," Ace commented.

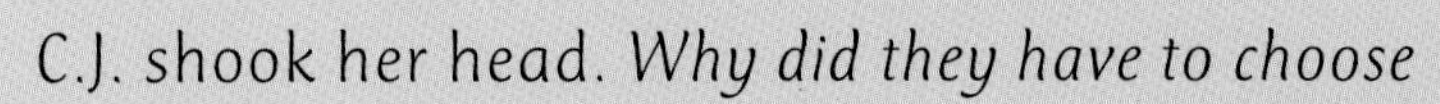

C.J. shook her head. *Why did they have to choose my beach?*

Over the next few days, C.J. kept running into Nick, Ace, and Yushi. Some mornings, she spotted them in their clubhouse. Afternoons, as C.J. dug her moat and designed her drawbridge, they bodysurfed on her end of the beach. They even asked her to join them. C.J. had been watching them and could tell they really looked out for each other. She couldn't help wondering what that felt like.

But C.J. had more important things to think about.

C.J.'s castle was taking shape. Any day now, a famous architect might walk by and notice her masterpiece. She thought about showing it to Nick, Ace, and Yushi. But they hadn't come by for a couple days.

So what? C.J. told herself. *I'm better off by myself.*

Yet she found herself listening for Nick's laugh or one of Ace's silly facts. And every time she saw a seagull, she thought of Yushi.

Finally, C.J. went looking for them. She figured they'd be in their clubhouse. But when she got there, they were staring at a pile of rubble.

"They killed our clubhouse," Yushi said.

Ace kicked at what had been their clubhouse door.

"Somebody wants to build a store here."

Nick stared up at C.J. "We don't have any place to meet now."

"I—I..." She what? C.J. felt bad for them. Part of her wanted to tell them they could share *her* clubhouse.

But that was crazy. This wasn't her problem. She was fine on her own, and they would be, too. "I'm sorry," she managed to say. Then she took off running.

C.J. didn't want to think about Nick and the others. Sitting alone in her hideout, she drew shapes in the sand. Maybe she could design them a new clubhouse. But they probably wouldn't want her help anyway.

After a while, C.J. heard voices outside. She hurried out to find Nick, Yushi, and Ace standing over her sandcastle.

Only the castle wasn't standing. It was ruined, smashed to a lump of sand. Yushi patted the castle's broken wall.

"C.J.?" Nick said.

"How could you?" C.J. screamed.

"Pardon me?" Ace asked.

C.J. refused to cry. "Just because I wouldn't let you use *my* clubhouse, you didn't have to knock down my castle!"

Ace shook her head. "We just came to invite you to—"

"Oh right!" C.J. snapped. "Get out of here—you *and* your God!"

Nick moved closer. "C.J., we'll go. But God's not going anywhere."

C.J. knew if they said one more word, she'd burst into tears.

“Just leave me alone!”

After they left, C.J. stared at her broken masterpiece. Now nobody would discover her. She dropped to the ground and fingered the shells that had formed her drawbridge.

That's when she saw them. Running through the middle of her castle were a dozen paw prints. "A dog did this?" she whispered.

Not Nick, Ace, or Yushi.

C.J. tore down to the water's edge. Nick, Ace, and Yushi were the closest things to friends she had. Now they'd never speak to her again—not after what she'd said.

C.J. stared at the sparkles of sun dancing on the ocean. The water made *swish-crash* music against the sand. It was so beautiful, a design, a masterpiece. "Did you do this, God?" She tried to remember everything she'd heard Nick's mom say about God and Jesus. What if it were all true? What if God had a purpose for *her* life? Was God the famous architect she'd been waiting for? Was God the one watching?

C.J. trudged back up the beach. She was almost to the lifeguard stand when she heard laughter. Yushi, Ace, and Nick were elbow-deep in wet sand, trying to fix her fallen castle.

ha ha ha ha ha ha ha ha h

Ace spoke first. "We *are* trying. But did you know that in all the world, there are no two castles exactly alike?"

C.J.'s throat felt dry as sand. "Thanks. And I'm really sorry, you guys."

They worked together the rest of the day. "You know," C.J. said, rebuilding the drawbridge while Yushi worked on the moat, "my lifeguard stand would make a pretty good meeting place. I kind of resigned from the C.J. Jones Club."

"Cool!" Nick answered.

When they finished, C.J. stood back and admired their sandcastle. It looked better than ever. "I still want to be an architect," she admitted. "Do you think God will let me?"

Nick grinned. "*Let* you? Who do you think made *you* so you *want* to build things?"

"Well, I'll be," Nick said, staring at C.J.

"What?" she asked.

"Don't look now, but C.J. Jones is smiling."

C.J. let it happen. It felt good to smile. And in her head, where she could sometimes picture the castles she was going to build, she could picture something else now. God.

And God was smiling, too.

DISCUSSION QUESTIONS

Made for a Purpose can help answer the big question, "What on Earth am I here for?" After you've read this book with your child, ask, "What purpose do you think God made you for?" to stimulate conversation. Perhaps ask an older child, "What gifts has God given you to help you become what he created you to be?"

Rick Warren's five purposes found in *The Purpose-Driven® Life* are listed below with discussion questions to deepen the child's understanding:

1. *You were planned for God's pleasure.*
   - Why do you think God smiles when you are doing what he made you to do?
   - Why do you think God smiles when you worship him?
2. *You were formed for God's family.*
   - Why do you think God created us to be with other people?
   - Why might someone be afraid to let you be their friend?
3. *You were created to become like Christ.*
   - How can you use the special talents God has given you to teach others about him?
4. *You were shaped for serving God.*
   - Why do you think God created us to help other people?
   - What are some ways we can help other people?
5. *You were made for a mission.*
   - Why do you think God wants us to tell the whole world about his love?